P9-CBE-426

Topic: Winter   **Subtopic:** Shapes

Notes to Parents and Teachers:

It is an exciting time when a child begins to learn to read! Creating a positive, safe environment to practice reading is important to encourage children to love to read.

REMEMBER: PRAISE IS A GREAT MOTIVATOR!

Here are some praise points for beginning readers:

- You matched your finger to each word that you read!
- I like the way you used the picture to help you figure out that word.
- I love spending time with you listening to you read.

Book Ends for the Reader!

Here are some reminders before reading the text:

- Carefully point to each word to match the words you read to the printed words.

- Take a 'picture walk' through the book before reading it to notice details in the illustrations. Use the picture clues to help you figure out words in the story.

- Get your mouth ready to say the beginning sound of a word to help you figure out words in the story.

Words to Know Before You Read

Christmas tree

circles

pointy

presents

round

snowman

squares

triangles

WHAT CAN I MAKE?

By Carolyn Kisloski

Illustrated by Srimalie Bassani

Rourke
Educational Media

rourkeeducationalmedia.com

What can I make?

I have two circles.

I can make a snowman.

Round, round circles.

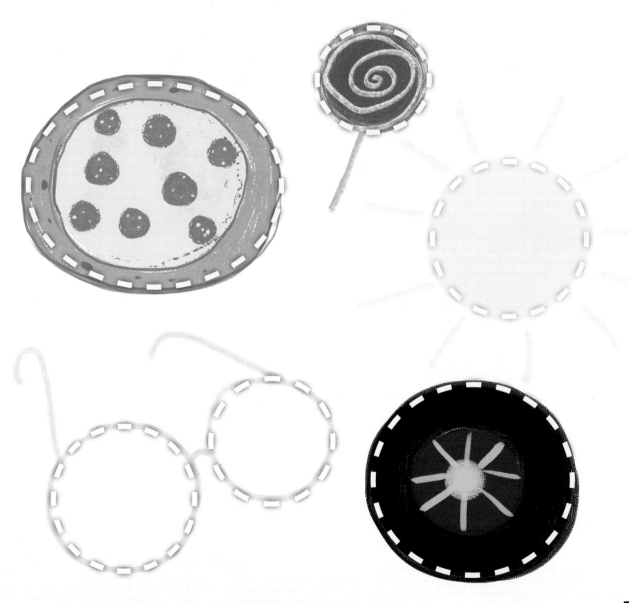

What can I make?

I have three triangles.

I can make a Christmas tree.

Pointy, pointy triangles.

What can I make?

I have four squares.

I can make presents.

Squares, squares, squares.

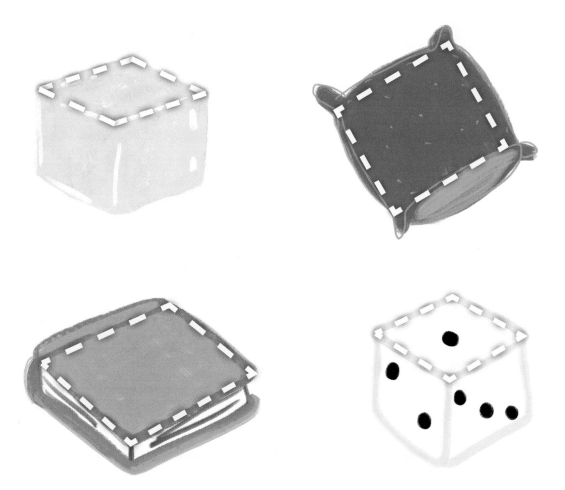

I have one star.

What can I make?

I can make a Christmas
tree star.

Pretty, pretty star.

Look at my Christmas card.

I will send it to you!

Book Ends for the Reader

I know...

1. What shapes does the snowman have?

2. How many triangles does the Christmas tree have?

3. Can you name two things the boy made?

I think ...

1. Have you ever made a Christmas card?

2. What do you want for Christmas?

3. What shape do you like best?

Book Ends for the Reader

What happened in this book?

Look at each picture and talk about what happened in the story.

About the Author

Carolyn Kisloski has been a life-long teacher, currently teaching kindergarten at Apalachin Elementary School, in Apalachin, NY. She is married and has three grown children. She enjoys spending time at the beach and the lake, playing games, and being with her family. Carolyn currently lives in Endicott, NY.

About the Illustrator

Since Srimalie was a child her mother gave her the passion for drawing and painting, and she had always encouraged her artistic expression. Her work is always full of surprises. It's difficult to remove her from her writing desk, where she keeps a stack of books, pages, tea cups of many colors and also amuses her fat cat.

Library of Congress PCN Data

What Can I Make? / Carolyn Kisloski

ISBN 978-1-68342-706-3 (hard cover)(alk.paper)
ISBN 978-1-68342-758-2 (soft cover)
ISBN 978-1-68342-810-7 (e-Book)
Library of Congress Control Number: 2017935352

Rourke Educational Media
Printed in the United States of America, North Mankato, Minnesota

© 2018 Rourke Educational Media

www.rourkeeducationalmedia.com

Edited by: Debra Ankiel
Art direction and layout by: Rhea Magaro-Wallace
Cover and interior Illustrations by: Srimalie Bassani